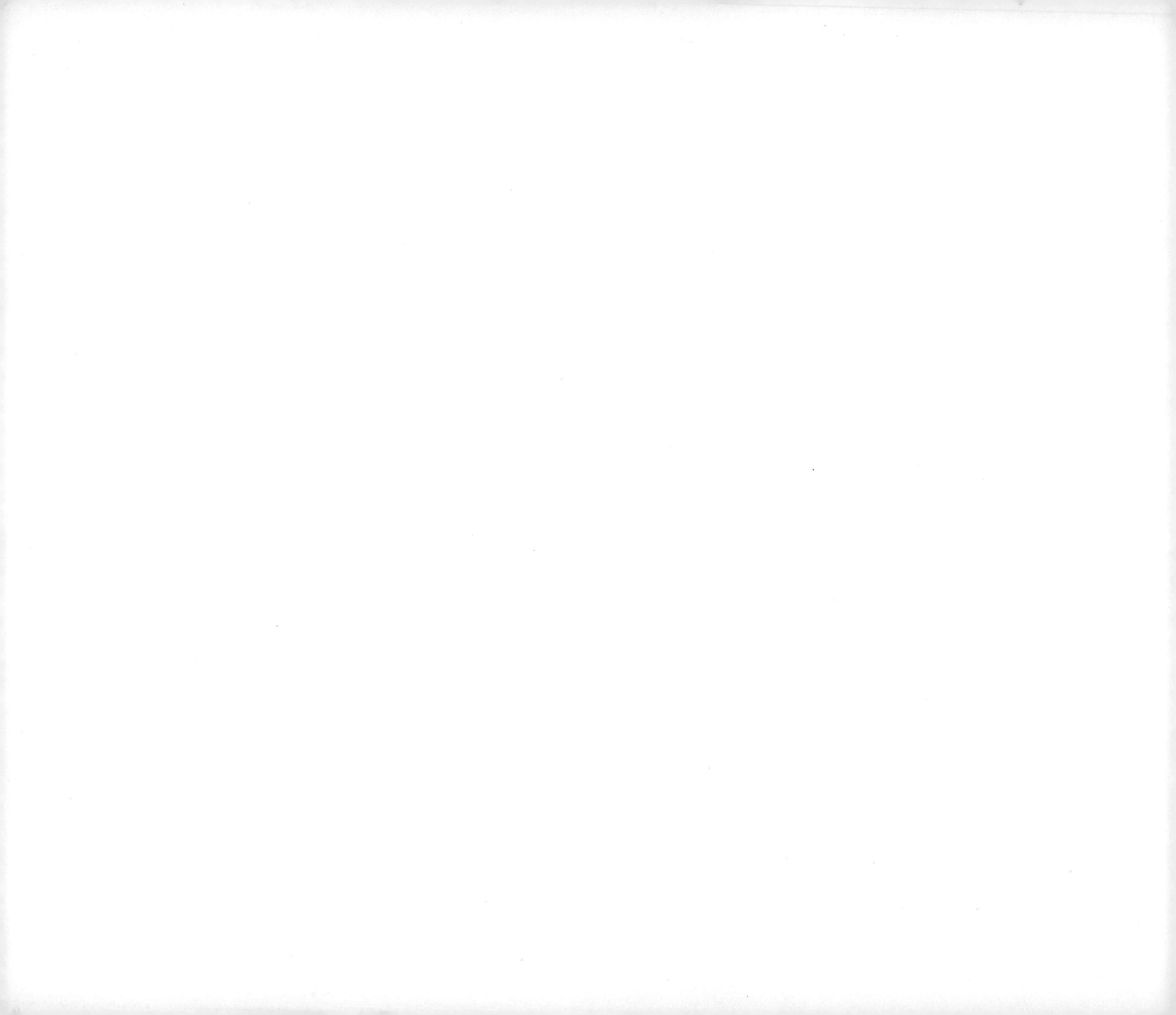

THE LONELY PHONE BOOTH

by Peter Ackerman *illustrations by* Max Dalton

DAVID R. GODINE · *Publisher* · *Boston*

First published in 2010 by
David R. Godine · *Publisher*
Post Office Box 450
Jaffrey, New Hampshire 03452
www.godine.com

Library of Congress Cataloging-in-Publication Data

Ackerman, Peter.
The lonely phonebooth / by Peter Ackerman ; illustrations by Max Dalton.
– 1st ed.
p. cm.
Summary: When cellular telephones arrive on the scene, a once-popular Manhattan phonebooth becomes shabby and lonely until a power outage reminds everyone of how useful it can be.
ISBN 978-1-56792-414-5
[1. Telephone booths–Fiction. 2. Loneliness–Fiction. 3. Cell phones–Fiction. 4. New York (N.Y.)–Fiction.] I. Dalton, Max, ill. II. Title.
PZ7.A18255Lon 2010
[E]–dc22
2010009372

SECOND PRINTING, 2013
Printed at Toppan Leefung Printing Ltd. in China

For Clea, Stanley, and Alvin

With special thanks to Peter Mendelsund

Once there was a Phone Booth on West End Avenue and 100th Street in New York City.

Everyone used it:

a businessman
always running late
for meetings,

a girl scout
who needed
more cookies,

a construction foreman
who needed cement,

a zookeeper who
lost his elephant,

a cellist who left
her cello in a taxicab,

a ballerina who wanted
to know if she got
the part in *Swan Lake*,

a birthday clown
who could never
find the party,

even a secret agent
who needed to
change his
disguise.

Sometimes
people had
to wait in
long lines

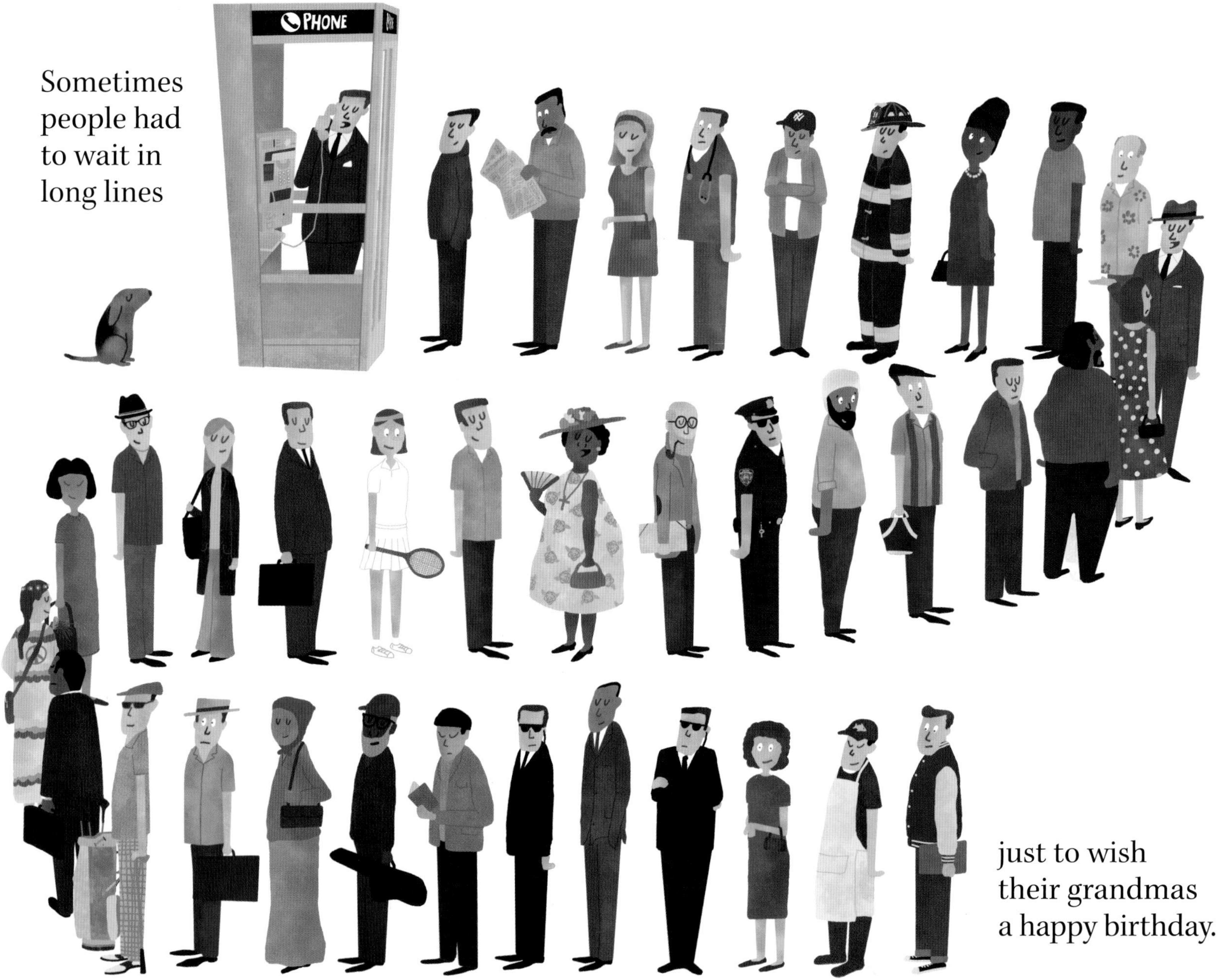

just to wish
their grandmas
a happy birthday.

Each week, phone company workers came to clean and polish the Phone Booth, to collect the deposited coins, and to make sure that its buttons were working properly.
The Phone Booth was very happy.

Then, one day,
the businessman
strode right past the
Phone Booth
and shouted into
a shiny silver object:

"I'll be there in ten minutes!"

The next day, the construction
foreman ran out of cement,
put a shiny silver object to his ear,
and fifteen minutes later,
the cement truck showed up.

On Thursday,
the girl scout
ran out of cookies,
pulled out her own
shiny object
(hers was pink),
and said, “We’ve got
plenty of Thin Mints.
Need more Tagalongs.”

“Who is
everyone
talking to?”
wondered the
Phone Booth.

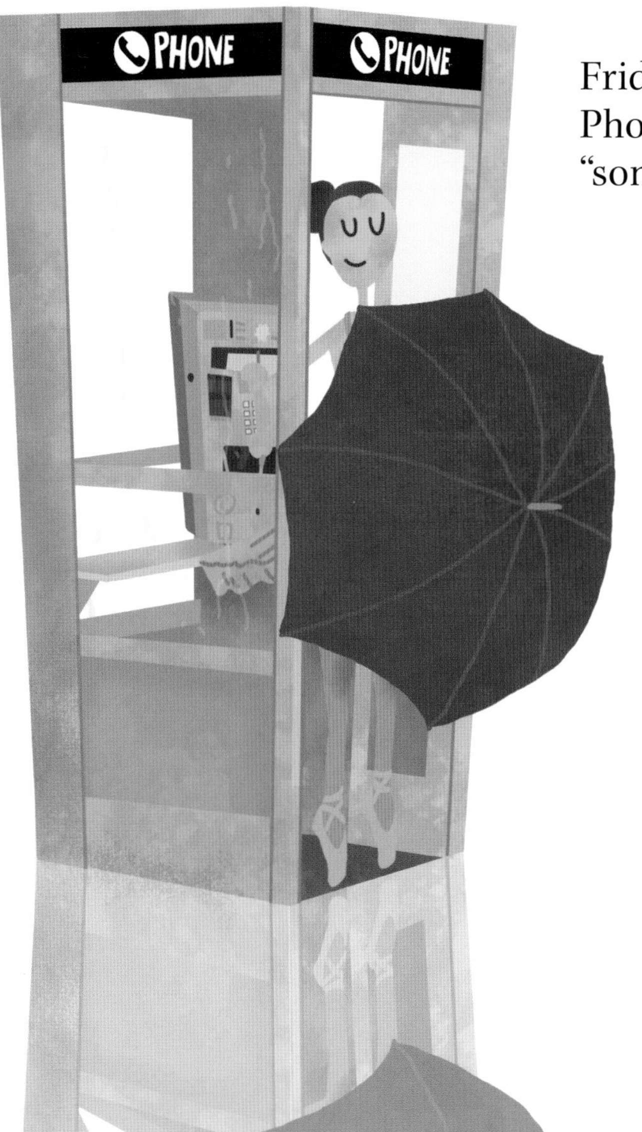

Friday it rained, and the ballerina dashed inside the Phone Booth's doors. "Finally," thought the Phone Booth, "someone remembers me."

But instead of taking the phone from the hook, the ballerina put a shiny object to her ear and said, "Well? Did I get the part?" The Phone Booth was flabbergasted.

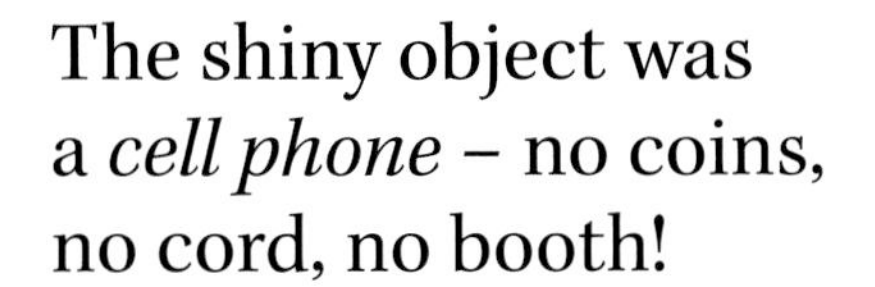

The shiny object was
a *cell phone* – no coins,
no cord, no booth!

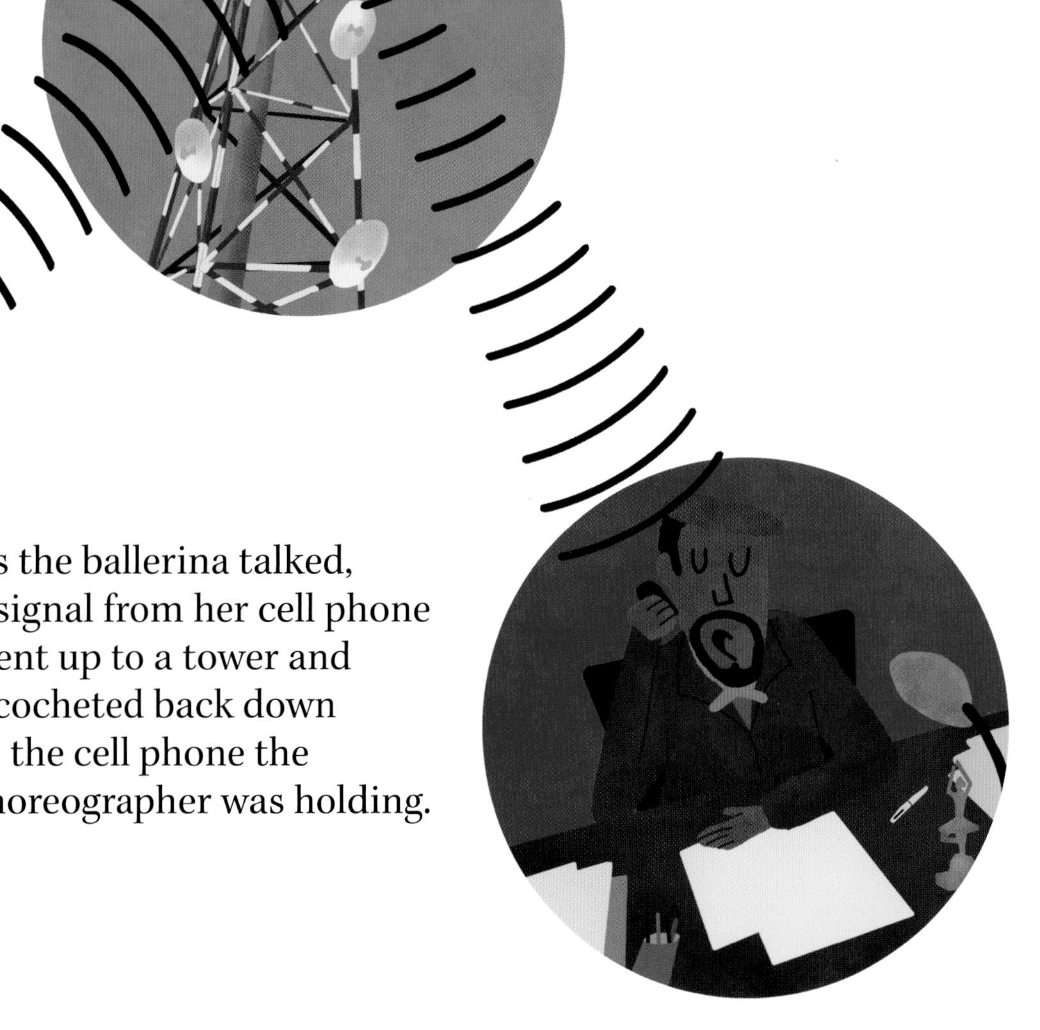

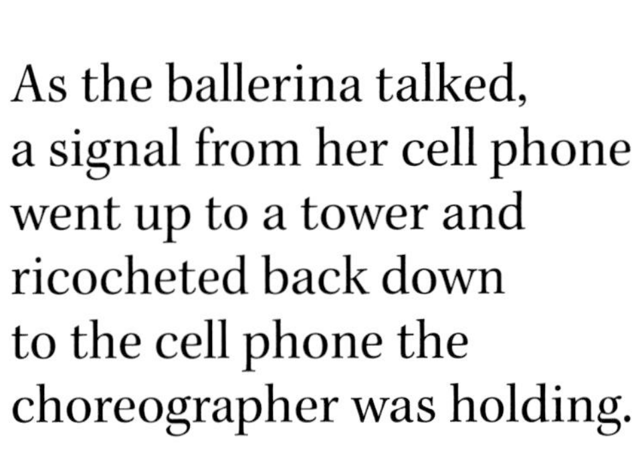

As the ballerina talked,
a signal from her cell phone
went up to a tower and
ricocheted back down
to the cell phone the
choreographer was holding.

The Phone Booth was devastated. "If people have their own portable phones, they won't need me anymore," the Phone Booth thought.

And it was right.

Soon no one used the Phone Booth,

not the zookeeper when he
lost his Wild African Dik-Dik,

nor the cellist when she left
her cello in the cab for
the eighty-thousandth time,

nor the grandma who wanted to
tell everyone it wasn't her birthday
so would they please stop calling her.

The workers who cleaned and polished the Phone Booth stopped cleaning and polishing it. Its hinges started to rust. Its paint started to peel. A window cracked and no one came to fix it.

The Phone Booth started looking so shabby that even the secret agent changed his disguise in the run-down hotel next door.

The Phone Booth became lonely.

It saw other phone booths carted away to the dump.
It knew that soon it would be carted away too.

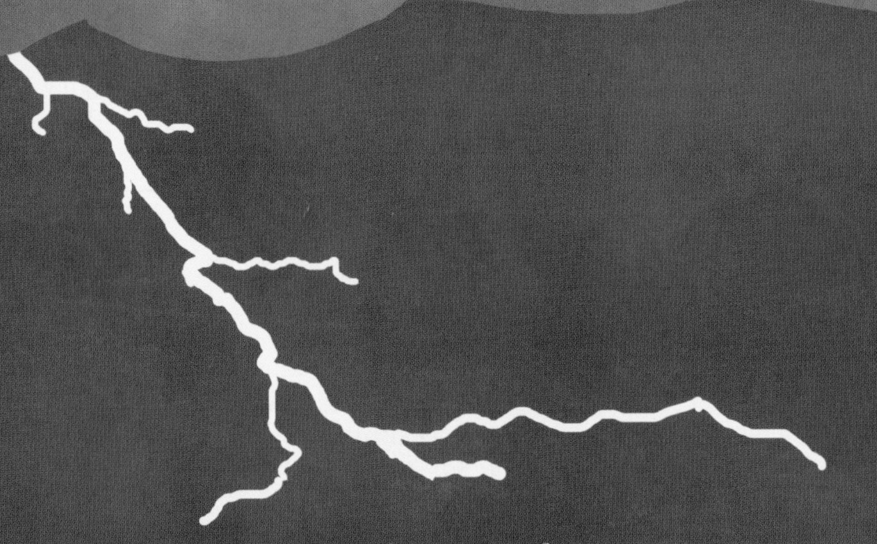

Then one day a great storm raged.
Lightning bolts split the sky and knocked out electrical wires,
shutting down the city.

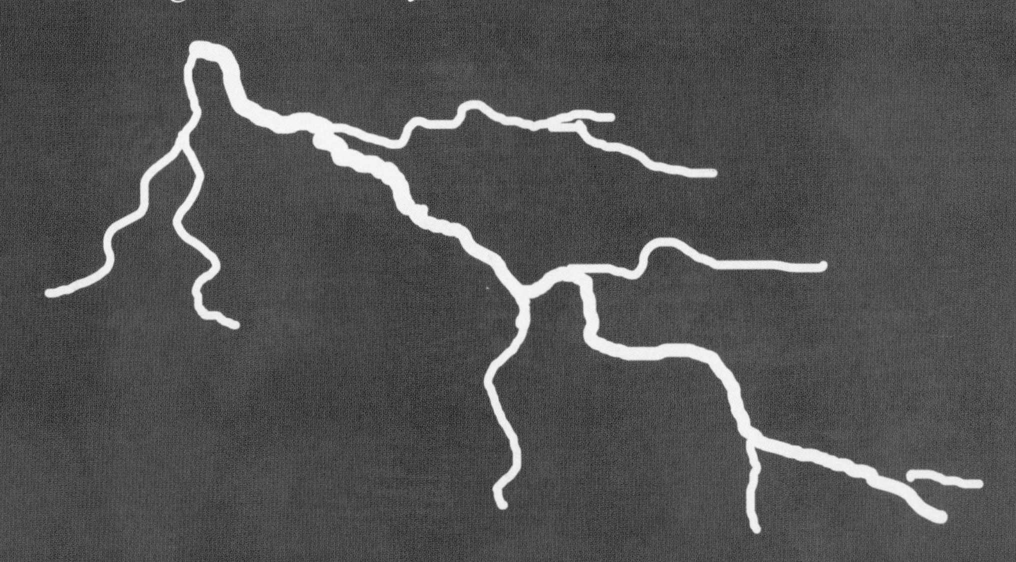

Everyone tried to use their cell phones at once and all the signals short-circuited the tower, causing each and every cell phone to go silent.

The people on the street had no way to call their friends, family and offices to let them know they were okay.

But the lonely Phone Booth still stood on West End Avenue and 100th Street.

"Hey, does this old thing work?" asked the construction foreman.

"I doubt it," said the clown.

"Let's see," said the girl scout.

She pushed open the rusty doors with a creak, lifted the phone from the hook, put a coin in the slot, listened for the click, pushed the buttons, and waited . . .

and *it worked!*

The people formed a line.
They blew aside the dust and coughed.
They ignored the Phone Booth's broken window…

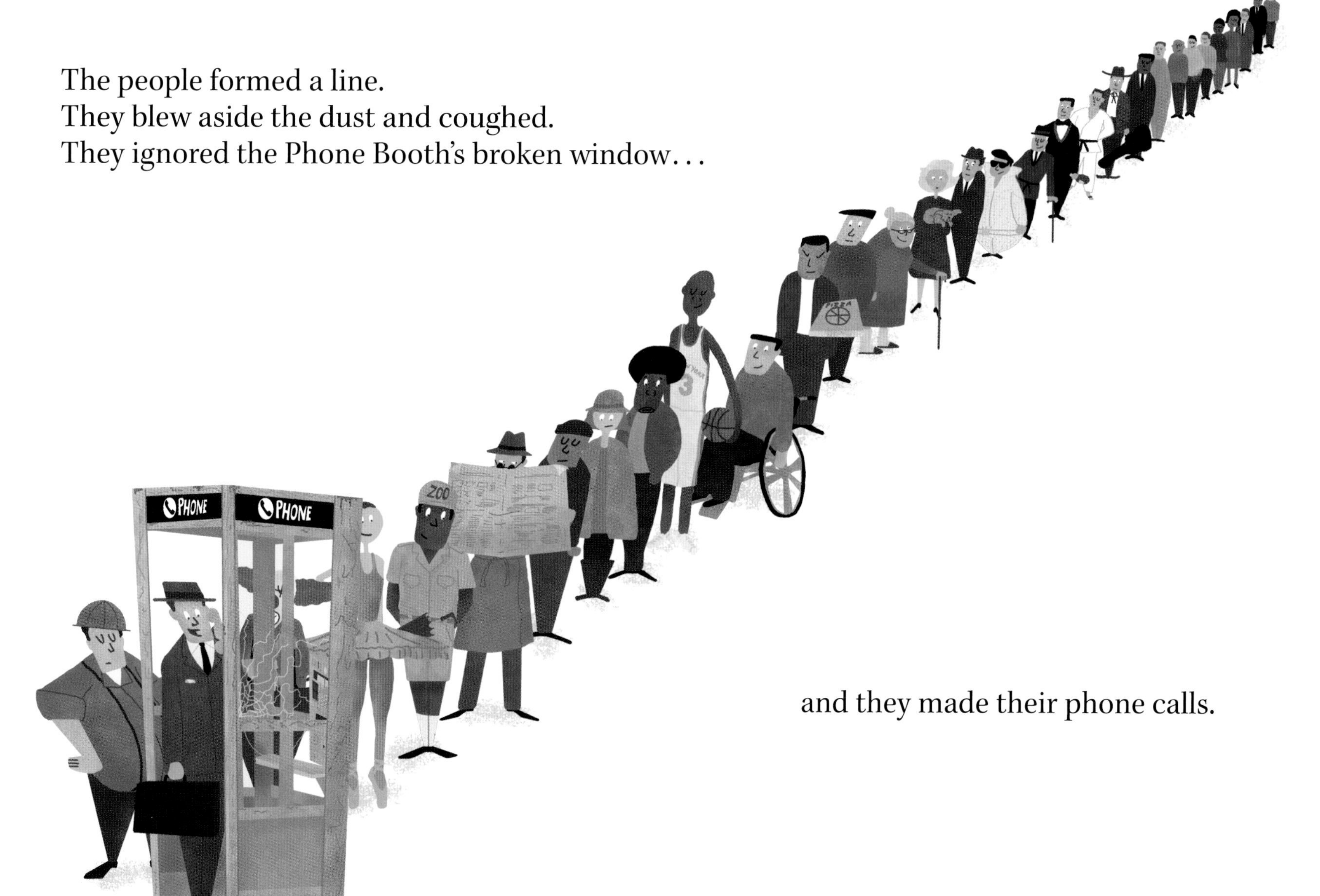

and they made their phone calls.

The ballerina called to see if she got the part in *Swan Lake*. She didn't.
But she did get the part in *The Nutcracker!*

The birthday clown called to see if the party was still on. *It was!*

The secret agent called his grandma
to wish her a happy birthday.

And the zookeeper called to say
he found the Wild African Dik-Dik
and the elephant in a poker game
on 103rd Street.

When the electricity
came back on,
the lonely Phone Booth
was lonely no more.

Phone company workers came to clean and polish it
and fix its broken window. They even had to collect
money from its coin box, which was overflowing.

The Mayor said the Phone Booth was
a hero and put up a plaque.

The Phone Booth was very happy.

But just then, city workers arrived
to cart it away to the dump.
The Phone Booth felt scared.

It could not shout, “Don’t cart me away!”
because although it could help one person talk
to another person, it could not speak for itself.
There was nothing the Phone Booth could do.

But the people of the neighborhood spoke up:

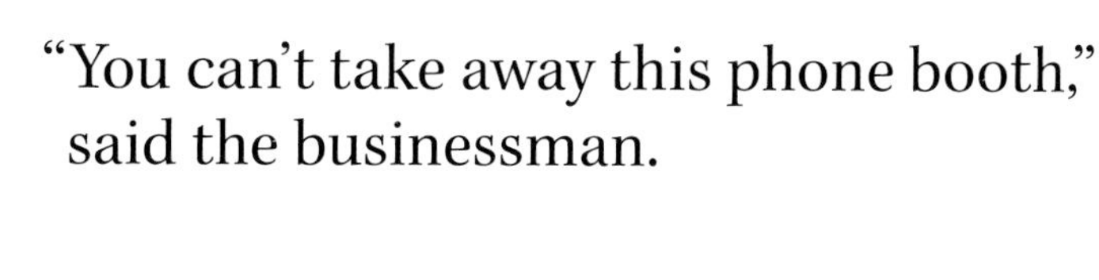

"You can't take away this phone booth," said the businessman.

"Yeah," said the girl scout. "It's part of the neighborhood."

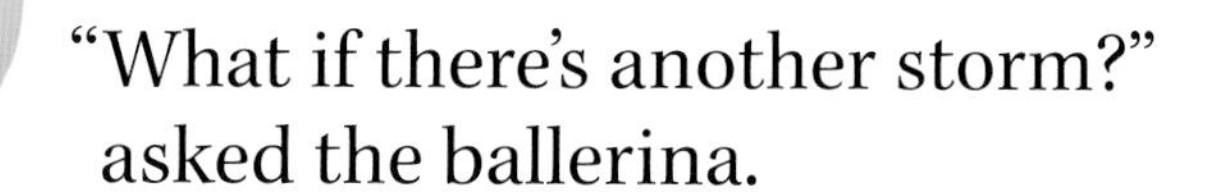

"What if there's another storm?" asked the ballerina.

"Or if I lose my cell phone in a taxicab?" said the cellist.

"What if the run-down hotel closes and I have nowhere to change my disguise?" asked the secret agent.

"It's been here forever," said the construction foreman.

"We love it," said the clown, shaking a rubber chicken.

Then the Phone Booth's phone rang.
It was the Mayor's grandma.

"Don't let them take down
that Phone Booth," she said.
"I remember when they put it in.
It's a national treasure."

The Mayor made the city workers drive away.
The people of the neighborhood cheered, hugged the Phone Booth, danced around it, and had a party.

And to this day, if you go to West End Avenue and 100th Street in New York City, you will see the Phone Booth.

Don't be shy.
Step inside,
lift the phone off the hook,
put a coin in the slot,
listen for the click,
push the buttons,
hear it ring . . .

and neither you nor
the Phone Booth
will be lonely
anymore.

THE END